Dedicated to all our
professors at SCAD

This volume collects From Scratch
For more stories go to www.sorcery101.net

Write Kel: sorcery101@gmail.com

ISBN: 978-0-9827864-0-6

Printed in USA

No.

That's not your problem

That's mine.

Your problem is that you're a complete and utter bluenose.

You always have been and always will be.

And yer an asshole.

Why are you always SO mean to me?

YOU **SHOT** ME.

It won't stick.

Loki...

I mean, it should. Loki

Loki!

For the past few centuries, demons have referred to me as a name, which roughly translates to DarkFire

Lately, to work with humans, I've taken the alias Mr. Tamura.

You may address me as either.

Ah think comin' here mighta been mistake.

OH?

Ah'm mostly usta dealin' with other vampires.

Not werewolves an' demons an'...

...whatever you are, Sir.

So, we are hired to execute a Mr. Zamboni and his most trusted men

Fortunately, most of our targets will be at a bachelor party...

...for Zamboni's nephew.

Sasha—

Despite your dissatisfaction with your role—

I still don't see WHY I gotta dress as as a maid.

Mr. Harper—

Why did Ah 'gree to this?

Because everyone wants to pull off a heist that is utterly perfect.

We're not stealin' anythin'.

We're not?

We're killing folks.

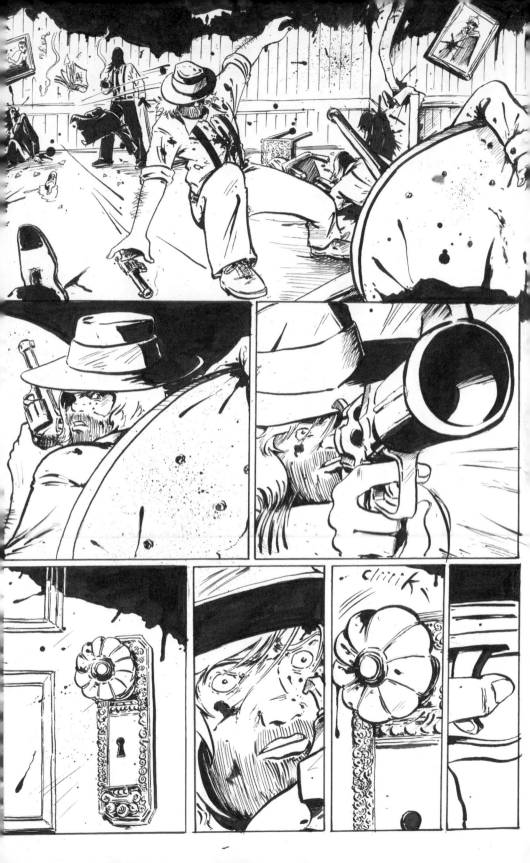

chitik

Why... Hello Loki. Hello, Aaron, wasn't it?

Yeah.

I see you took care of things here.

And you handled a few on your own too.

Yes, however I accidentally blocked the restroom.

I have to move them so I can wash up before leaving.

Oh- Yer an ice demon.

From my understanding, humans seem to find blood stains disconcerting.

We were looking for clean clothes.

.Good.

A few other human men left with some less covered human women.

If you find them during your search,

Please kill them.

okie dokie

Yes. Ah think.

Then you are better at your job than Seth was.

Good work. If you would like, you are welcome to continue accompanying us.

Uh....

Are you talking about me while I'm not here?

Worry not. I'm fine.

GRR!!

I do not think it would even occur to me to be worried about your well-being.

We were merely discussing how Aaron is better suited to watching Loki than you.

# Fun Facts About the Book

- All the signs are referencing people Jose and I know in real life.

- Jose uses FW ink

- Kel can draw too (see ad on next page)

- After the first scene, Jose said, "Kel, it's the 20s. Everyone smokes in the 20s. Can I add more smoking in this?" I told him okay. So, on almost every page after, Jose made it his personal challenge to have smoking on every page.

- Most of the main cast has appeared in other comics Kel wrote. Jose got pictures of them with notes on their personalities, mannerisms, and heights. Kimaya and Sasha and the mobsters were designed completely by Jose.

- Jose really likes ketchup.

- Kel really likes sushi.

- Jose draws the pages at 8 inches by 12 inches (roughly 20.3 cm by 30.5 cm)

- The original script for the comic was 50 pages.

Read more comics by Kel McDonald at
www.sorcery101.net
You might see a few familiar faces!

See more of Jose's Artwork at
www.joe-pi.com